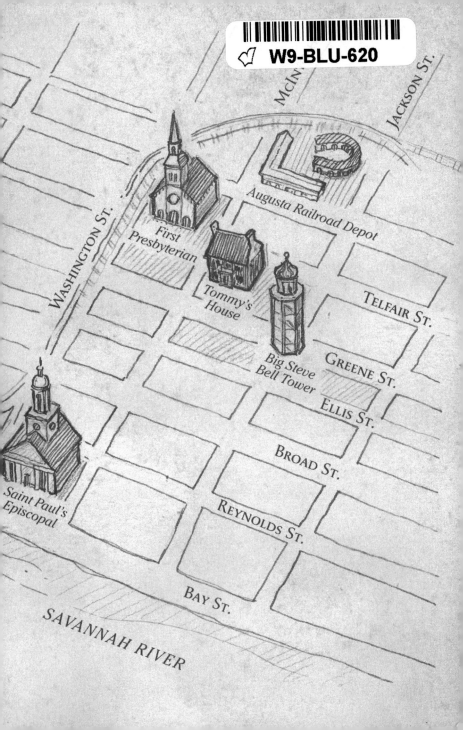

McIN...

JACKSON ST.

Augusta Railroad Depot

First
Presbyterian

WASHINGTON ST.

Tommy's
House

TELFAIR ST.

Big Steve
Bell Tower

GREENE ST.

ELLIS ST.

Saint Paul's
Episcopal

BROAD ST.

REYNOLDS ST.

BAY ST.

SAVANNAH RIVER

ESCAPE by NIGHT

A Civil War Adventure

LAURIE MYERS

illustrated by AMY JUNE BATES

SQUARE
FISH

Henry Holt and Company ❋ New York

For SDG

The author would like to acknowledge the assistance
of the Porter Fleming Foundation.

SQUARE
FISH

An Imprint of Macmillan Publishing Group, LLC
175 Fifth Avenue
New York, NY 10010
mackids.com

Square Fish books may be purchased for business or promotional use.
For information on bulk purchases, please contact the Macmillan Corporate
and Premium Sales Department at (800) 221-7945 x5442 or by e-mail at
specialmarkets@macmillan.com.

Library of Congress Cataloging-in-Publication Data
Myers, Laurie.
Escape by night : a Civil War adventure / Laurie Myers ; illustrated by
Amy June Bates.
p.   cm.
ISBN 978-1-250-05055-7 (paperback) / ISBN 978-1-4299-7496-7 (e-book)
1. United States—History—Civil War, 1861–1865—Juvenile
fiction. [1. United States—History—Civil War, 1861–1865—Fiction.
2. Conduct of life—Fiction.   3. Christian life—Fiction.]
I. Bates, Amy June, ill.   II. Title.
PZ7.M9873 Es 2011   [Fic]—dc22   2010030117

Originally published in the United States by Henry Holt and Company
First Square Fish Edition: 2014
Book designed by Véronique Lefèvre Sweet
Square Fish logo designed by Filomena Tuosto

5   7   9   10   8   6   4

AR: 3.8 / LEXILE: 520L

Contents

Augusta, Georgia

October 1863

CHAPTER 1

The Book

The dog's ears stood straight up. He rushed to the window and barked loudly.

"What's bothering Samson?" Annie asked, looking up from her book.

Tommy pushed open the second-story window and leaned out. Samson joined him.

"There's a wagon coming down Telfair Street," he said. "Samson, what do you think's in the wagon? Hogs?" Tommy smiled as he imagined the hogs snorting and squealing.

"It's more likely beans or squash," Annie said. She tossed her book aside and joined them.

The wagon rolled by, and the awful scene below left them speechless. Instead of colorful vegetables or squealing hogs, the cart overflowed with dirty, bloody Confederate soldiers. They looked like old rags that had been cast aside. A breeze carried the unmistakable stench of sickness and death up to the window.

"Oh, my," Annie said, covering her nose and mouth.

Samson's nostrils flared.

"Smells like rotten fish," Tommy said. "They must be going to our church."

First Presbyterian Church, where their father was pastor, stood catty-corner to their house.

The white picket fence surrounding the church shone in the noonday sun. "I wish they wouldn't use our church as a hospital," Annie said.

"It's still a church," Tommy said.

"Not with that yellow flag flying out front. Yellow flag means hospital."

Tommy turned his attention back to the wagon.

"Look, the man on top is missing an arm."

The one-armed man stared into the sky with a strange blank look on his face. Tommy looked up to see what held the man's attention. Clouds whirled around like giant balls of white yarn unrolling across a deep blue sky.

"The men aren't moving," Annie said.

Tommy and Annie had seen a lot of wounded men coming and going from the railroad depot. Those men were constantly moving, hoping for

some relief from their pain. The only movement on this cart was one man's lifeless leg, which hung off the back, swinging back and forth like the pendulum of a large clock.

"You think they're dead?" Tommy asked.

"That would explain the smell. I bet they're on their way to Magnolia Cemetery."

Tommy pointed. "Look, the one-armed man has something under his arm."

Annie squinted. "It's a book—maybe a Bible."

"Or secret battle plans," Tommy whispered.

Just then, the small ragged book slipped out from under the man's arm and landed on the edge of the wagon. The wagon hit a bump, and the book bounced into the middle of Telfair Street.

"He lost his book!" Tommy said.

Annie shrugged. "The man is dead. He won't miss it."

The cart slowed. The driver motioned to two soldiers standing in front of the church. They disappeared inside and returned with a stretcher, then carried the one-armed man inside.

"See? He's *not* dead," Tommy said. His voice reflected the pleasure he felt at his small victory over Annie.

"I hate war," Annie said. "I'm going to the cookhouse to see what's for lunch. Come on, Samson."

Samson stared at Annie but did not move.

"Why won't he come?" she said. "And for that matter, why does he always sleep in your bed? I want him to sleep in mine."

Annie stared at the unmoving dog. "All right. Stay if you like, but you're my dog, too." She left the room.

Tommy stared at the small, dusty book in the middle of the street.

"That book must be special if the soldier carried it through the battlefields all the way to Augusta," he said to Samson. "If you think we should get the book, then *bark*."

Samson barked.

"Good boy." Tommy put his arm around the dog. "I can't go outside until after lunch. Mother said so. That means if we want the book, it's up to you to *fetch*."

Samson whined.

"That's right. *Fetch*."

Samson followed Tommy down the stairs. Tommy opened the front door.

"*Fetch* the book."

Samson trotted down the steps and into the street. He picked up the book and returned to Tommy. They hurried to the sitting room, where Tommy inspected the cover.

"There's no title or author's name, Samson.

Should I open it? I can't read words very well, but there might be maps inside. I can read a map."

Samson pulled at Tommy's arm.

"What's the matter? You don't want me to open it?" Tommy stared at the small leather strap that held the book closed. He wanted to tear it open, but something held him back. He rubbed the book as if to bring out its secrets.

"Maybe you're right," Tommy said. "This might be important for the war. I should return it to its owner."

Tommy gazed out the window at First Presbyterian Church. He had gone inside only once since it had become a hospital. The bright, well-kept sanctuary was gone; in its place was a world filled with screams, groans, and pleas for help, and a heavy, overpowering smell of death.

"Samson, I'll return it. But I'm not going inside the church by myself. You'll have to go, too."

At the word "go," Samson stood.

"Not yet," Tommy said. "After lunch we'll find the one-armed man."

CHAPTER 2

The One-Armed Soldier

Tommy held the book tightly under his arm as he and Samson crossed the street toward the church. A train rumbled down Washington Street, heading for the depot.

"That's the third train today," Tommy said. "They're carrying more soldiers to North Georgia, so the war must be getting worse."

Tommy climbed the steps into the stone archway of the church. Samson stopped.

"Come on, Samson."

Samson did not move. He had not been allowed in the sanctuary, and that memory remained strong. It didn't matter that Reverend McKnight had given him permission. "If it provides those young men even the smallest comfort, then I believe the Lord would not mind," he had said. Samson was not convinced.

"Come," Tommy said firmly. Samson came.

They sucked in one last breath of fresh air and entered the sanctuary. Tommy surveyed the room. It wasn't nearly as bad as he remembered. Light poured in through the tall windows that lined the walls, giving the place an almost cheery feel. The surgeons and nurses hurried from man to man, comforting one, delivering a cup of water to another.

The rows of cots did not seem so out of place today. The day they had removed the pews and set up the cots, Tommy and his sisters, Annie and Marion, had climbed into the pulpit and counted every cot—220.

"Master Tommy." It was Henry, one of Mr. Barrett's slaves. Mr. Barrett, a banker, was a mean and stingy man, but for the sake of the Confederacy, he let Henry work at the hospital.

"Tommy, what's a big ten-year-old boy like you doin' here? You ten now, ain't ya?"

"Almost."

"Almost? Don't you be addin' years. Life do that all by itself. If you're looking for the Reverend McKnight, he's over there."

Across the room Reverend McKnight sat in a

chair, his Bible open in his hands. He was a tall man and easy to spot, even when seated. The sight of his father gave Tommy confidence.

"I'm looking for a soldier with one arm," Tommy said.

"Lots of men here have one arm."

"He just came in," Tommy said.

"Then he's yonder by the pulpit."

Tommy stuck close to Henry as they walked between the rows of cots.

"Come here, pup," a man called.

Samson glanced the man's way but stayed near Tommy.

Then Tommy spotted the one-armed soldier on a cot near the corner. A thin stream of light poured onto him from the window above.

"Is he going to be all right?" Tommy asked.

"Only the good Lord knows for sure."

Henry led Tommy to the man's side. Through the blood and dirt they could see his skin, pale as biscuit dough. He didn't look too old. His beard was just a light stubble.

Samson circled a few times, then settled into a ball under the cot. Mrs. Williams came out of nowhere, a basin of water balanced on her hip and a book under her arm. She served as president of the First Presbyterian Ladies Sewing Circle.

"I must have this soldier's name," declared Mrs. Williams.

Tommy thought he saw the man's eyelid twitch. He clutched the book and watched the man closely. "He's asleep," Tommy said.

Mrs. Williams scanned the room. "Keeping up with all these boys is downright impossible."

"If he wakes up, I'll ask," Tommy offered. The man's eyelid twitched again.

Mrs. Williams handed the basin to Henry. "Here's water so he can clean himself."

After she left, Tommy knelt for a closer look. Suddenly the man's eyes popped open.

"Ha," Tommy said. "I knew you were awake."

CHAPTER 3

A Commonplace Book

"Where am I?" the man asked. His soft voice had an accent, but not like the German or Irish people in Augusta.

"You are in First Presbyterian Church in Augusta, Georgia," Tommy said. "I'm Thomas McKnight, but they call me Tommy. This is Samson. He's a greyhound."

Samson came out from under the cot at the

sound of his name. He looked the man directly in the face, then stepped forward to accept a pat.

Tommy smiled. "Samson likes you. My father says a dog can tell a man's character."

"I think your father's right." Turning to Henry, the man asked, "Who are you?"

"Henry."

"I'm pleased to meet you, Henry."

Henry smiled and looked down. "Thank you, sir," he said.

Tommy had never heard a white man use a formal greeting with a slave.

"What is your name, sir?" Tommy asked.

"Redmon. Redmon Porter. Most people call me Red."

Red scanned the room. Samson did the same. Tommy looked too, but all he saw was a hospital full of Confederate soldiers.

"Are you looking for someone?" Tommy asked. "'Cause if you are, I could help."

"I'm not looking for—hey, where'd you get that book?" He pointed to the book still tucked under Tommy's arm.

"It fell off the cart," Tommy said.

"Did you read it?"

"No, sir," Tommy said, pleased he could answer truthfully. He handed the book to Red, who pressed it to his chest. He relaxed, as if the book itself were medicine.

"It doesn't have a title," Tommy said.

"It's my commonplace book. You write anything you want in it."

"Read us something," Tommy blurted out. He knew it sounded impolite. He should have asked.

"Well . . ." Red's hesitation made Tommy even more interested.

"Why not?" Tommy asked. "You're not going anywhere."

"Henry, can I trust this boy?"

"Yes, sir, Mr. Red. Tommy McKnight is a fine boy. His father is the pastor of this church."

Tommy held his head high, waiting to be taken into confidence.

"Okay, I'll read you something special. It's a poem that I wrote just before the Battle of Chickamauga."

Using his one hand, Red fumbled to find his place in the book. Henry reached to help him, but Red said, "No, I'm going to learn to manage with one hand." He balanced the book on his chest and read:

"I only tell the stars above the longing of my soul:

To fight till death in early morn to
make a nation whole.
God, can this be in your design or in
your perfect plan
To place the price of victory at even
one gentleman?
Fearfully and wonderfully you've
made each one so brave
To fight again just one more time,
though he may see the grave.
But I shall trust your sovereign hand
and continue in my path
Knowing that your just reward is in
the aftermath."

Tommy was silent. He had hoped for a secret
battle plan or information about a general coming
to visit Augusta, maybe even General Lee. Instead

he'd heard a poem. He had listened carefully to the words, just like his father taught him, and there was something unusual in the beginning.

"Will you read the beginning again?" Tommy asked.

"I only tell the stars above the longing of my soul: To fight till death in early morn to make a nation whole—"

"Wait," Tommy said. "Make a nation *whole*? We are fighting to be a separate nation."

"Some are fighting to keep the nation whole," Red said. He turned to Henry. "What do you think?"

"Don't know much about poems, but it sounded mighty fine to me. And I like that beginning!"

Tommy stared at Henry as if he'd said he was going to be president.

"I place a great trust in those to whom I read," Red said.

"You can trust us," Henry said. He stepped forward. "Let's get you cleaned up, Mr. Red. You got dirt on you from all across Georgia and parts beyond."

Red closed the book and stuck it under his leg.

CHAPTER 4

Big Steve

Tommy watched as Henry removed Red's jacket and put it under the cot.

"Your jacket's too big," Tommy said.

"It's all they had," Red replied.

Henry wet the washcloth in the basin and handed it to Red, who worked quickly. The water turned dark as he washed.

"Does that hurt?" Tommy asked.

"The wound doesn't hurt, but I feel pains in my arm, even though my arm's not there. It hurts like the dickens."

"Henry, I need you over here," called Dr. Harold.

"Comin'." Henry handed the basin to Tommy.

"When you come back, we'll talk," Red said as Henry left.

Red was almost finished and looking much better when Big Steve rang.

"That's Big Steve, our fire bell," Tommy said. "It rings every day at noon to remind us to pray. It rang one hundred times when South Carolina . . . What is that word for leaving the Union?"

"Secede," Red said.

"That's it. It rang one hundred times when South Carolina seceded. And it rang all day when Georgia seceded!"

"I guess everybody was pleased," Red said.

"Yes, but not anymore," Tommy said.

Red lifted the washcloth from the basin and let the bloody water drip off. "War is not as pretty as people thought." He tossed the dirty washcloth into the bowl and lay back. "Tell me about Henry."

"He belongs to Mr. Barrett," Tommy said.

"He's not a free Negro?"

"No. There are free Negroes in Augusta, but not Henry."

"Do you think Henry wants to be free?" Red asked.

"Yes," Tommy said, without hesitation. "Henry has someone telling him what to do all the time. I hate it when my sisters tell me what to do."

The last ringing faded away. They were so engrossed in the soothing sounds that they did not notice Tommy's father's arrival.

"I'm Reverend McKnight," he said, extending his hand to Red.

Red's hand seemed to disappear in Reverend McKnight's large hand. They shook, but Red remained silent.

"Can you talk, son?"

Red shook his head no.

"He was talking a minute ago," Tommy said.

"Tommy, our young men go through a lot. If they don't want to talk, they don't have to."

Reverend McKnight looked thoughtfully at Red, then stooped down and pulled Red's jacket from underneath the cot. He ran his fingers over the buttons.

"I noticed the buttons are Mississippi. I met some Mississippi soldiers this summer."

Red shifted nervously.

"Father, I thought you were with Georgia soldiers."

"I served as chaplain for the Confederate States of America, not just Georgia. I ministered to whomever the Lord God brought across my path."

Red was silent.

"Let me pray for you, son." Reverend McKnight closed his eyes. His facial expression indicated that he was discussing the most important situation in the world with God. He placed his hand on Red's shoulder.

"Father God, we ask your healing hand on this, our brave brother. May he cast his cares upon you and find comfort in your arms . . ."

As Tommy listened, he wondered about Red. Why wouldn't Red talk to his father? Tommy did not know a single person who did not like his father. And Red treated Henry differently, not like a slave. And that line in the poem about making a nation whole? What did that mean?

No doubt about it, there was something different about Red. But Tommy liked him anyway. He liked that he treated Henry well. Mr. Barrett certainly didn't. He liked Red's poetry too, in spite of that odd line.

As Tommy considered Red, a nagging thought would not leave his head. And if it was true, it would be serious—life-and-death serious. One way or another, Tommy needed to find out the truth.

CHAPTER 5

Blessed Are the Peacemakers

Tommy walked home from the hospital with his father. Samson glided along beside them.

"Father, remember at the beginning of the war, how excited everyone was, and all the parades on Broad Street?"

"Yes, there was great hope for victory."

"Well, I don't think war is exciting," Tommy said. "I think war is terrible."

"Indeed it is," said Reverend McKnight. " 'Blessed are the peacemakers' has new meaning for me these days."

"Father, what happens to Yankee prisoners?"

"Some are traded back to the North in exchange for our men, but most are sent to prison until the war is over."

"I heard Dr. Harold say there's not enough food and the prisoners are starving," Tommy said.

"That could be. Food shortages are everywhere."

Tommy nodded. "Mother sent me out for sugar yesterday, and I couldn't find any."

"Sugar is about as scarce as a burp in a prayer meeting," Reverend McKnight said.

Tommy laughed. Reverend McKnight stopped at the steps. "You coming?"

"No, I'm going to stay out here with Samson."

Reverend McKnight nodded, then his long legs took the steps two at a time, and he disappeared into the house.

Tommy sat on a step while Samson stood alert like a soldier ready to hear the battle plan.

"Samson, I'm thinking about something, and it's serious."

Samson gave Tommy his full attention.

Tommy lowered his voice. "I'm not sure Red is a Confederate soldier."

Samson moved closer.

"I know what you're thinking, Samson. What else could he be? Well, I think he might be a . . . Yankee."

The word hung in the air, like a cannonball ready to crush them.

"I know he doesn't look like a Yankee," Tommy said. "But did you hear his accent? He sounds different, like he's not from around here, or not

even from the South. And his jacket . . . I know it's from Mississippi, but it's way too big. And that line in his poem about making the nation whole. *Yankees* want to make the nation whole."

Samson placed his head in Tommy's lap.

"The whole idea is crazy," Tommy said. "A Yankee hiding out in Augusta? In First Presbyterian Church? Right across the street from our house!"

Tommy scratched the dog's ears. "Maybe my mind is just running away with me. That's what Mother says. But somehow we have to find out. Are you with me, Samson?"

Samson wagged his tail.

"Good. Tomorrow we'll investigate."

CHAPTER 6

Troubled

"It is my turn to read," Annie announced, as if it were a biblical truth.

With her short dark hair parted down the middle, Annie looked like Mrs. McKnight.

"It is Marion's evening to read," Mrs. McKnight said.

"Marion may be reading tonight, but tomorrow

it's my turn, and nobody better try to take my place," Annie said.

Tommy knew no one in the room was foolish enough to try that.

"What are we reading?" Tommy asked.

"*History of the Covenanters in Scotland,*" Marion said.

Everyone in the family loved those stories. The British government wanted to conquer the Covenanters, who were heroic Christians from Scotland. It was kind of like the Yankees trying to take over the South, Tommy thought.

Reverend McKnight walked in. He turned up the gaslight on the wall. "Tommy, I found this outside." He held up a baseball. "With all the refugees in town, things are likely to disappear."

Reverend McKnight pretended to be a pitcher. His long legs and arms whirled around like a windmill as he tossed the ball to Tommy.

Tommy caught it and Reverend McKnight yelled, "Out!"

"Joseph," Mrs. McKnight said, suppressing a laugh.

"We couldn't let the runner get to first," he said, giving her a peck on the cheek. "Marion, you better get us started before the runner heads to second."

Marion smoothed back her ringlets, then began reading in a soft, tension-filled voice.

Tommy had chosen a seat by the window. It was not the most comfortable seat in the room, but he could see the church. Samson curled up under the chair.

The family listened as the Covenanters scattered throughout the countryside.

Tommy turned his attention to the church. The corner of the churchyard appeared to be filled with fireflies, more than Tommy had ever seen, flashing their lights on and off, on and off. He looked closer. It was only a few of the hospital patients standing outside smoking their cigarettes.

"Bang!" Marion yelled as a Covenanter shot a government soldier.

Tommy wished he could be like the Covenanters—heroic and brave. If Red really was a Yankee, Tommy could expose him and be a hero. He imagined Robert E. Lee stepping off a train at the Augusta depot and shaking Tommy's hand while the citizens of Augusta cheered.

With great feeling, Marion read the final words of a soldier to the minister: "You owe your life to this mountain."

Then, in a perfect minister's voice, Marion read the reply. "Rather, sir, to that God that made this mountain."

Marion closed the book and said, "The end."

"Marion, that's not the end," Reverend McKnight said.

"Well, I want a happy ending. A book is the only place to find a happy ending nowadays."

"Yes," Annie said. "The war is ruining everything. You have to wait in line forever at the store, and then they don't have half of what you want."

"When the war started, everyone said it would not last more than two months," Marion said. "It has been going on for over two years!"

"Father, how is the war going?" Tommy asked.

They could tell by Reverend McKnight's face it was not good.

"The Yankees are almost in Georgia."

Marion threw up her hands. "Next thing you know, they'll be in Augusta!"

Tommy held his breath.

"Is there news from Atlanta?" Mrs. McKnight asked.

"The fighting is in the mountains now. If the North is victorious there, I fear the entire state will be lost. And if Georgia is lost, the Confederacy can scarcely survive."

Mrs. McKnight gasped.

"You mean we might lose?" Tommy asked. This was something he had never considered. It was one of those impossibilities, like flying horses.

Marion straightened in her chair. "We are troubled on every side, yet not distressed. That's Second Corinthians."

"Very good," Reverend McKnight said.

Tommy glanced out the window again at the church. He felt troubled on every side, and distressed too.

CHAPTER 7

A Dream

Tommy stood at the entrance to the sanctuary with Samson and Annie.

"We have to get rid of Annie," he whispered to Samson.

"Don't talk behind my back," warned Annie. "I have very good hearing."

Tommy spotted Mrs. Williams and waved. She bustled over.

"Tommy, that soldier friend of yours still isn't talking, at least not to the white folks."

"What soldier friend?" Annie asked.

"No one," Tommy said.

Mrs. Williams pointed across the room. "See, he's talking to Henry again. Tommy, go tell Henry to get back to work."

"Yes, ma'am," Tommy said.

Mrs. Williams led Annie away. "There's a soldier I want you to read to."

Tommy made his way across the room. He could see Henry and Red talking intently, like they were planning some major battle strategy.

Henry hopped up when he saw Tommy. "I best be gettin' back to work," Henry said.

Tommy thought Henry looked nervous, but decided it was because he had been caught talking instead of working.

"Take a seat," Red said to Tommy.

Tommy searched Red's face for some sign that he was a Yankee, but saw nothing.

Red grimaced and rubbed his upper arm briskly. "My stump sure hurts, but I'm better off than most." Red wiggled his right fingers to show their vitality.

Tommy noticed Annie several rows over, reading to a soldier who looked asleep.

"You're quiet today," Red said.

"Just thinking," Tommy said.

"About what?"

"I was wondering why you wouldn't talk to my father."

"I didn't feel much like talking. That's all."

"I'd like to hear more from your book," Tommy said. "Unless there are things in there you'd rather me *not* hear."

Red studied Tommy. "No, I'll read more, but like I said, I put a trust in the people to whom I read."

Red reached for the book, but it had fallen on the opposite side of the cot.

"Samson, *fetch* the book," Tommy said.

Samson went around the cot, picked up the book, and offered it to Red.

"Smart dog," Red said.

"Watch this," Tommy said. He turned to face the dog. "If you want to hear Red read, *bark*."

Samson barked.

"Good dog," Red said. He opened the book. "I'll read you a dream I had on the battlefield."

A man on a nearby cot was softly playing a fiddle, and it seemed to Tommy like the perfect music for a dream.

"I am traveling down a long road covered with leafy trees. I am carrying something fragile, and all around me is danger. I come to a big hole in the road, and I cannot pass. A sadness comes over me, because my mission might fail."

Red paused.

"Go on," Tommy urged, but Red would not be hurried.

"Out of the woods steps an angel. The angel shows me a bridge. If I cross, my mission will be complete."

Red stopped.

"Did you cross the bridge?" Tommy asked.

"I don't know. The dream ended."

"What was the dream about? Were you on a mission?"

"You could say that."

"What was the big hole?" Tommy asked.

"An obstacle."

Tommy's heart beat faster. "And danger is all around you." He swept his arms out to take in the entire sanctuary.

"That's right."

Tommy couldn't stand it any longer. He blurted out, "Are you a Yankee?"

Red's eyes did not leave Tommy's face. His answer was simple. "Yes."

For a moment, Tommy was speechless, then he whispered loudly, "You aren't supposed to be here. This is the South!"

"I didn't have much choice in the matter."

Tommy studied Red. "You look like a regular person."

"I am. I just want to get back to my family in Ohio. Tommy, I have a two-year-old little boy I haven't seen in over a year. I need an angel."

"Like in the dream?" Tommy said.

"Yes," Red said. "I have to get out of here soon. That Mrs. Williams keeps asking questions. Next thing you know, some Mississippi boys'll be here, and I'll be found out. Will you help me?"

"That's against the South," Tommy whispered.

"Tommy, it's not right to keep another person as a slave. Men should be free."

Tommy paused. He had thought about the states being free, but not the slaves.

"Some slaves are happy," Tommy said.

"Is Henry happy?"

Tommy could not think of anything good about living with Mr. Barrett. Mr. Barrett was constantly yelling at all his slaves, not just Henry. It would be miserable to live with him.

"We're not fighting about slaves," Tommy said. "We're fighting because the North is trying to tell us what to do. States should be free." It didn't sound nearly as good as when he'd heard Marion say it.

"Some folks may not be fighting about slavery, but I am. Slavery is wrong, and I'll give my life to stop it."

CHAPTER 8

Great Power

"Red may be a Yankee, but I still like him," Tommy told Samson on the way home. Samson pushed his head into Tommy's hand.

"I guess I'm supposed to turn Red in. But if I do, they might send him to a prison camp. I've heard terrible things about those places."

"Master Tommy!" Henry caught up with Tommy and Samson.

"You and Samson talkin' serious. Don't forget now. Mercy is a great power," said Henry.

"Father preaches about mercy. God gives us mercy, even though we don't deserve it," Tommy said.

Henry nodded. "He sure does. And you know what God expects of you?"

"What?" Tommy asked. That was exactly what he had been wondering.

Henry leaned forward like he was revealing a deep secret. "Micah. Chapter six."

Tommy thought hard. Micah was a book in the Old Testament. He knew that much. But that was all he remembered.

Henry recited the passage. "What doth the Lord require of thee, but to do justly, and to love mercy, and to walk humbly with God?"

"You know as many Bible verses as Father," Tommy said.

Henry smiled big, showing a row of bright white teeth. "It's the power to help you live right."

"You make it sound easy," Tommy said.

"Loooooove mercy, Master Tommy. That's all." Henry smiled and walked on down Telfair Street.

Henry always smiled, even when things went badly for him. Tommy recalled once a couple of years ago when he and Samson were waiting for his father outside Mr. Barrett's bank. Henry was sweeping the brick walkway. Mr. Barrett kept yelling at him to hurry up. It looked to Tommy like Henry was working as fast as a man could. When he was almost finished, some older boys passed by and kicked dirt onto his clean walk. They laughed like it was the funniest thing in the world.

Mr. Barrett had been watching from the window, and Tommy thought he would chase the boys away. Instead, he charged out with his rifle and pointed it at Henry. Then he cocked it. Samson growled. Tommy held him tight. Henry didn't move. Finally, Mr. Barrett barked, "Get it clean." Then he laughed and went back inside.

Henry had whispered to Tommy, "I'm waitin' for the blessed hope."

"Are you going to tell?" The sharp voice brought Tommy abruptly back to the present. He wheeled around to see Annie with that I-know-a-secret look on her face.

"Are you going to tell?" she demanded again.

A bad feeling washed over Tommy. He thought back to the hospital. Several times he had seen Annie watching them. She might have heard what they were saying if she had made an effort, which Tommy now thought she had.

"Tell what?" Tommy asked, trying to sound innocent.

"You know." Annie looked back at the church as if the building itself were guilty.

Tommy looked too, half expecting to see the devil standing at the door.

"Annie, there is nothing to tell." Tommy was sure he sounded guilty.

"Tommy, we are at war, and we cannot have Yankees parading around as Confederates. If you don't tell, I will."

Her words hit like a hammer. She whirled around and started up the steps.

"Annie, wait. I have a deal for you."

She stopped. "What kind of deal?"

Tommy thought quick. "A good deal."

"What kind of good deal?"

Tommy was silent.

"Tommy, you don't have a deal. You are just stalling for time."

"Maybe I am, and maybe I'm not. Maybe I have a really good deal, and you don't know it."

"All right. I'll give you till tonight. And the deal better be good, or I'm telling." She marched up the steps and into the house.

Samson had found a bone and was working on it by the steps. Tommy sat down beside him.

"Samson, we're in trouble. We have to come up with something to keep Annie quiet. And on top of that, I'm not even sure we should help Red."

Samson abandoned his bone and gave Tommy his full attention.

"Remember when the war started? Everyone said how bad the Yankees were."

Samson stared at Tommy.

"I thought Yankees were bad, too. Maybe some are bad, but I don't think Red is. All he wants is freedom for people like Henry. And to tell the truth, I like the idea of Henry being free."

Samson gave his bone a sideways glance.

"If I were Henry, I'd want to be free," Tommy said.

He picked up the bone and handed it to Samson, who anchored it between his paws and began working on it with his back teeth.

"If we don't help Red, he might go to prison. But helping wouldn't be easy. And it's against the law, so I'm not even sure we should."

Samson paused from his work on the bone.

"Whatever we do, Samson, we need to keep Annie quiet. And I think you just might be the answer."

CHAPTER 9

The Deal

Annie sat on the sofa fluffing out her dress, like she was the queen and Tommy was her subject.

"Pleeeease don't tell," Tommy pleaded.

"Tommy, you heard Father last night. We are on the verge of losing the war."

"One Yankee is not going to matter," Tommy said.

"I'm not so sure about that."

Samson came in. Sensing the importance of the conversation, he sat erect between the adversaries and followed the conversation with his head.

"Just promise you won't tell, at least until tomorrow."

Annie refluffed her dress. "I cannot make such a promise."

Tommy said, "Yes, you can. Open your mouth and say, 'I pro—'"

"Tommy, stop it. You said you had a good deal. Now, let's hear it."

"I'll let Samson sleep in your bed," Tommy said.

Annie stopped fluffing. "For how many nights?"

"One week."

"A week? Hmm."

"Annie, Red has a two-year-old little boy, and he hasn't seen him in a year."

Annie's brow wrinkled.

Mrs. McKnight came in. "I'm sorry to be late. More refugees came in today. And as if that weren't enough, I was on the other side of the tracks and had to wait for a train to pass." She removed her bonnet. "Your father has a meeting tonight, so he will not be here for reading. Annie, I believe it is your turn."

"I don't feel like reading," Annie said, giving Tommy a sideways glance.

"You love to read," Mrs. McKnight said. She eyed her children. "What is going on?"

Tommy held his breath. At any moment, Annie was going to tell everything. It would pour out, like rain running off the roof.

"Come on, Samson," Tommy said. "Sit over here by Annie."

Samson moved to Annie's side and snuggled in close.

Annie brightened. "I changed my mind. I will read."

Tommy heaved a sigh of relief.

Annie pranced across the room to the bookshelf. Tommy did not know what caused her to hold her tongue. Perhaps it was the silent prayer he'd said, or maybe just her love of dogs. Whatever the reason, at least now he had more time to think about what to do.

The next day was Sunday. Ever since First Presbyterian Church had been turned into a hospital, the congregation had met at the Baptist church a few blocks away. Tommy decided he would make his decision Sunday morning.

CHAPTER 10

Streams of Mercy

Tommy had not slept well. The weight of the situation was growing heavier. He had heard Henry say, "The heaviest burden in the world is a burden carried alone." Henry was right.

The Baptist church gave Tommy a peaceful feeling. He sat in the pew between Marion and Annie. Their mother sat by Annie. They were waiting for the service to begin when Mrs. Williams marched up. In one long exhaled breath, she said, "Tomorrow they are bringing in more wounded from Atlanta—hundreds of them."

"Oh, my," Mrs. McKnight said.

Mrs. Williams lifted her arms into the air like she was asking the congregation to rise. "Where will they put them? Every hospital is packed."

She turned to Tommy. "I hear there are some Mississippi boys in the group. Maybe your soldier will finally have some friends."

Tommy felt squeezed, and it had nothing to do with the crowded pew. Between Mrs. Williams, Annie, and the Mississippi soldiers, Red would likely be discovered, and soon.

Reverend McKnight began the service with a reading from Psalms. Everyone stood. Normally, Tommy would have listened. Today he could not concentrate. Questions exploded in his head like fireworks. Should he tell someone about Red? Should he help Red? Should Red go to prison? The enemy was supposed to go to prison. But Red didn't seem like the enemy.

"Surely goodness and mercy shall follow me . . . ," Reverend McKnight read.

Mercy. That's what Henry had talked about.

Tommy looked back at the slaves' section of the church. Henry was sitting on the front row. He gave Tommy a nod.

Everyone sat down.

Did Red deserve mercy? Mercy was not something you deserved. It was a gift.

Reverend McKnight began the morning prayer. "Gracious Father, we enter into your presence . . ."

What would God want? Tommy thought. God was a God of grace and mercy—he'd heard that all his life. Would God want Red to go to prison, or home to his family?

Marion punched Tommy in the side. The congregation was standing to sing. Tommy stood.

What did God expect him to do? What were those three things from the book of Micah? To do justly, love mercy, and walk humbly with God. Love mercy.

"Streams of merrr-cy, ne-ver ceeea-sing . . ." The congregation sang, and the words leaped out at Tommy. Streams of mercy, never ceasing. That's what God wanted. Not a little mercy here and there, but streams of it, running on and on like the Savannah River. Suddenly it was clear what he should do.

Tommy looked at his father high up in the pulpit, singing with passion as he always did. The congregation was singing loudly too, and with joy. Tommy felt relief for the first time in two days.

As soon as church ended, Tommy found Henry.

"I know what you mean about mercy," Tommy said.

Henry smiled. "What you gonna do?"

Tommy hesitated. His decision was a serious one, and he sensed the importance of secrecy. Henry of all people would understand, and even agree, but Tommy held back. "I'll tell you tomorrow." He added to himself, "If I'm not in jail."

CHAPTER 11

The Branded Hand

Tommy and Samson entered the sanctuary by the side door. Red was a few rows over, sitting beside an older man, holding his hand. Red spotted Tommy and slipped away to the side door. They stepped outside onto the stone steps, and Red took a deep breath.

"Fresh air smells good," he said. Then he saw Tommy's face. "What's wrong?"

"There are a lot of soldiers coming in tomorrow, some from Mississippi."

"I'll leave tonight. We're close to South Carolina, aren't we? I know some people there who'll help me get north."

Tommy frowned. "You'll have to cross the Savannah River to get to South Carolina, and it's too dangerous to swim."

"Is there a bridge?"

"Yes, there's a footbridge, but it's upriver and they started guarding it a couple of months ago."

"What about railroad trestles?"

"There are two. They're covered, so you could cross without being seen, but you have to get to the river first."

Tommy's heart beat faster. Red would have to cross every main street in Augusta: Greene Street, Broad Street, and Reynolds Street.

"I'll take you," Tommy said.

"No. I don't want you to get into trouble. It's enough that you're not turning me in."

"You can't make it by yourself," Tommy said. "You've never been to Augusta before. It'll be dark. You might run into trouble or get lost."

"I don't know . . . ," Red said.

"I know yards to cut through," Tommy said, feeling more certain than ever. "I can take you as far as Saint Paul's Church. It's right beside the river."

"I'll need clothes and food."

"I can bring them," Tommy offered.

"Can you meet me at eight?"

"Yes. My parents are going out visiting tonight. They'll be gone by then."

"Good. I'll be waiting."

A gentle breeze blew by, and for a moment it felt like their problems floated away. Red pulled his commonplace book from his pocket.

"I want to read you two lines from a poem. But first I'll read you the story of the man in the poem."

Red found the page he was looking for.

"A man, Jonathan Walker, who lived in Florida, moved his family to Massachusetts so his children would not be raised in the poisonous environment of slavery."

He emphasized the word "poisonous," and Tommy wondered if Red thought Augusta was a poisonous environment.

"Mr. Walker returned to Florida for a visit, and some slaves he knew, who had been members of his church, asked if they could go back to Massachusetts with him. He consented, and they left in a sailboat.

"They were two weeks out when a Southern ship caught them. Mr. Walker was imprisoned in a dungeon for a year, and the palm of his right hand was branded ss for slave stealer."

Tommy turned his own hands over and stared at the palms.

"The poem is called 'The Branded Hand,' by John Greenleaf Whittier. These lines are my favorite.

"*Then lift that manly right hand,*
bold ploughman of the wave!
Its branded palm shall prophesy,
' Salvation to the Slave!' "

The story was as compelling as the Covenanters.

"Is he alive?" Tommy asked.

"Yes, and he travels around giving speeches and showing off his hand."

"Lots of famous people come to Augusta on the train. Do you think he might come here?" Tommy asked.

"I don't think Mr. Walker would be welcomed." Red lowered his voice. "Someone else is coming with me tonight."

Tommy felt his pulse quicken.

"Another Yankee?"

He thought back to the soldiers he had seen in the hospital. None of them looked like Yankees, but neither did Red.

"For now, the less you know, the better it is for you. You'll see tonight."

CHAPTER 12

The Escape

Samson sat alert. All day long he had known something was going on, and he had not left Tommy's side.

Tommy sat on the edge of his bed, staring at a watch he had borrowed from his father's bedroom. Beside him lay a small sack with the things Red needed for the journey. Tommy reviewed the contents: an old shirt of his father's

from the mending pile and some food, which had not been easy to get.

Old Mettie, who worked for them, guarded the cookhouse closely these days. At supper Tommy had begged for extra biscuits, which he hid in his pockets. Later he managed to get some apples and carrots. At the time, it seemed like a lot. Now, it didn't look like much.

"It's five minutes till eight, Samson."

Samson stood.

Tommy clutched the sack like a security blanket as he tiptoed down the stairs. Samson stayed close at his side. Tommy peeked out the window. The street looked empty. They slipped outside and ducked behind a bush.

The wind blew gently through the trees and sounded like people whispering. Tommy thought of his father and mother, who had left an hour ago. By this time they would be in the Martins' home. How comforting it would be to sit with them now! Tommy shivered, unsure if it was nervousness or the cool fall air. He pulled Samson's warm dog body against him.

Tommy turned his attention to two soldiers who stood in front of the church. When they turned away, he and Samson dashed across Telfair and worked their way up McIntosh Street, moving in and out of the shadows. They crossed McIntosh and hurried to the side door of the church.

As quietly as possible, Tommy pushed open the door. The only light inside came from a couple of lanterns, which cast odd shadows around the tall room. Tommy had never seen the sanctuary look so scary. With the low moaning and restless shifting of soldiers, it reminded him of an Edgar Allan Poe story Marion had once read to him.

Red met them at the door, and they slipped outside.

"Here's the shirt," Tommy said.

With Tommy's help, Red quickly slipped it on. They walked to the back of the church to avoid the guards. The Augusta depot looked dark and frightening, stretching off to the right behind the church. Lately, the depot had been a place of constant activity, but tonight the trains stood dark and motionless.

Red stopped and put his finger to his lips. Footsteps. Tommy heard them, too, behind the church. It might be the soldiers from the front or some hospital patients strolling around the back. Neither was good.

Red and Tommy crouched at the corner of

the building. They didn't have time to wait until the footsteps faded away.

Tommy pulled Samson close and whispered softly in his ear, "See if anyone is there." He gave Samson a slight push, and the dog walked slowly around the corner.

CHAPTER 13

Hunting a Slave

After a minute Samson returned.

"The coast is clear," Tommy whispered. "If anyone was there, he would have barked."

Quietly, they made their way along the back of the church to the opposite side. The Medical College building across the street looked quiet.

"Which way?" Red asked.

Tommy pointed across the street to the live

oaks, standing strong and tall, like soldiers guarding the way. Tommy and Red dashed to the trees. Then, as normally as possible, they began to walk down Washington Street toward Saint Paul's Episcopal Church and the Savannah River.

They passed a few strangers along the way. At any moment Tommy expected one of them to yell, "Hey, that boy and his dog are helping a Yankee escape!" Tommy pushed the thought from his head and focused on their goal: the river.

Red walked briskly. Tommy and Samson kept up. Tommy felt more confident.

They were almost at Greene Street when, without warning, a dog leaped out at them. A small fence kept him at bay, but the fierce barking and snarling caused Tommy to stumble and fall. Almost immediately, a woman in her nightdress came to the door of a house.

Red quickly crouched behind the fence by

Tommy and Samson. A low growl rumbled in Samson's throat. Tommy held him close and stroked his neck.

"Stay down," Tommy whispered to Red. "I know her, and she's nosy."

"What in creation is bothering you?" the woman yelled. "Yankees?"

Her dog barked again.

"Well, there aren't any Yankees around here. I'm the one you better worry about." With that, the woman went back inside.

Tommy got up, glad he could rise without help. He rubbed his hands against his pants.

"You all right?" Red asked.

"Yes, sir," Tommy said, hoping he sounded confident.

In the distance a soft whistle blew.

"A train," Tommy said, "coming from South Carolina."

"How far?" Red asked.

"I can't tell, but we better hurry. There's not enough room on that trestle for you *and* a train. If you're on the trestle when the train comes . . ."

"I understand," Red said. He rubbed his stump.

They walked quickly past the next houses and were crossing Greene Street when Mr. Barrett rushed around the corner, nearly knocking them over. He held his rifle in both hands like he was hunting.

"Ah, young Tommy," he said. "I'm looking for Henry. That worthless excuse for a slave is missing."

"We haven't seen him," Tommy said, eyeing the rifle.

"I'm on my way to round up some help," Mr. Barrett said. Then he noticed Red.

"Tommy, do you have family visiting? I don't recall your father mentioning it."

"Pardon me," Tommy said. "This is my mother's cousin, Mr. Redmon Porter."

Red bowed slightly and extended his hand.

Mr. Barrett shook it. "Sir, I am Wallace Barrett. Unfortunately, I must excuse myself. I am in search of a missing slave. And if he's on the run, he'll be sorry when I get hold of him."

Mr. Barrett walked away without so much as a good-bye.

"We must hurry," Red said.

"But what's going to happen to Henry?" Tommy asked.

"Henry's the one we're meeting," Red said.

CHAPTER 14

The Diversion

Red explained that this was Henry's chance for freedom. Mr. Barrett had been watching Henry like a hawk, so Red had told Henry to meet them at Saint Paul's.

Tommy wanted to be happy for Henry, but he was awash with fear. Mr. Barrett was the meanest, most determined man in town. And he shot off his rifle at the slightest thing, good or bad.

With Mr. Barrett roaming around carrying a rifle, none of them were safe.

Tommy and Red hurried on to Ellis Street. They kept their heads down as they crossed. It was good practice for Broad Street, which would be the busiest and most dangerous place for running into people they knew.

"If we go through Mary Ellen's backyard, we can avoid the crowded part of Broad Street," Tommy said.

"Which way?"

"Follow me."

Tommy cut between two houses. He could hear the voices on Broad Street, less than a block away. He wondered if that was the usual amount of noise or if Mr. Barrett was already organizing his hunting party.

"That's the Wilsons' house," Tommy said, hoping to distract himself. "Their cat only has three legs. That's Mary Ellen's house. She's my sister Annie's friend."

They slipped along the edge of the yard, then stepped out onto Broad Street. It was bustling with people. The gaslights flickered along the street, making everything appear less sharp. Tommy hoped it might keep people from noticing them. He quickly scanned the crowd and felt relief at all the unfamiliar faces.

Two more blocks and they would be at Saint Paul's. Red would cross the river and be out of Augusta. Then this would all be over. Tommy hurried across the street. Red and Samson followed. They were continuing quietly through an alleyway to Washington Street when they heard the sound of pounding footsteps behind them.

"In here," Red said.

They ducked between two houses. It was a tight space. Tommy was close to Red and could

smell his shirt. It smelled like Reverend McKnight. Suddenly Tommy longed to be with his father, feeling his strength and confidence.

The footsteps grew closer. This might be it. Someone, maybe Mr. Barrett, had figured it out. Now he was coming for them. That's when Tommy heard a familiar voice whispering, "Tommy. Tommy, where are you?"

"It's Annie!" Tommy exclaimed. He emerged from the shadows. "What are you doing here?"

"I went to get Samson to sleep in my bed, and you were both gone. I figured this was what you were up to. I'm not stupid."

She stared at Red. "You don't look like a Yankee."

"Annie!" Tommy said.

"Well, it's true. He looks quite normal."

"You didn't tell anyone, did you?" Tommy asked.

"No. I want him to get back to his little boy.

Besides, one Yankee won't matter." She smiled at Tommy.

Big Steve began to ring.

"We must go," Red said.

"Don't worry," Annie said. "That's just Big Steve ringing. I saw Mary Ellen on Broad Street. She said Mr. Barrett is upset because Henry is missing. They're alerting everyone and starting a search on Reynolds Street."

Red looked at Tommy. "Is that where we're going?"

"Yes," Tommy said. He thought quickly. "Annie, we need your help."

"Doing what?"

"We need you to distract the men."

"How?"

"Take Samson with you. Go up Reynolds Street. When you get to the boat docks, tell him to bark. He'll do it. Keep him barking. When the group asks what's wrong, tell them you think you saw Henry running toward Telfair Street. That will send them in the opposite direction and give Red a chance to get across the river."

"I can do it," Annie said, her face set.

Tommy threw his arms around Annie for a quick hug.

She smiled. "Come on, Samson. We've got a job to do."

"Go, Samson," Tommy said.

Annie and Samson dashed off.

The train whistle blew again.

"Hurry," Tommy said.

CHAPTER 15

The Jubilant Bell

Time was critical. If the plan didn't work, the search party would be on them in no time. They stepped out of the alleyway onto Washington Street.

"There it is!" Tommy said. Saint Paul's stood majestically before them with its bell tower shining in the moonlight.

The train whistle blew again. Tommy and Red raced down Washington.

They paused at the corner and looked up Reynolds Street. They could see the brightness of lanterns moving toward them.

"I don't see Annie," Red said.

"She should be coming out any minute," Tommy said.

They stared into the darkness. The lanterns grew brighter; the voices of men, louder.

A gun went off, and Tommy jumped.

"That's the direction Henry will come from. Do you think they got him?"

Red shook his head. "Henry's a smart man. If anyone can make it, he can."

"There's Annie," Tommy said.

They could barely make her out in the distance. Then they heard barking.

"That's Samson," Tommy said. His heart filled with pride.

Samson barked and barked and barked again.

"Good dog," Tommy whispered. "Good boy."

The lanterns stopped, and the pride turned to fear. Men's voices grew even louder.

"What are they saying?" Tommy asked.

"I can't hear, but they're talking to Annie."

"Red, what if they don't believe her?"

"I trust Samson. Listen, he's still barking. He's putting up a big stink. They have to think something is wrong."

A man in the group suddenly yelled, and the group turned.

"They're headed in the opposite direction," Red said. "I knew we could count on that dog of yours."

Tommy and Red ran across Reynolds Street and collapsed in the bushes beside Saint Paul's.

They crawled on hands and knees along the side of the church until they reached the corner.

They peered out of the bushes. There before them stood two giant railroad trestles, like gray monster snakes slinking their way to South Carolina.

"You better go," Tommy whispered. "The train is coming, and those men could be back any time."

"I can't leave without Henry," Red said.

"What if Henry didn't make it?" Tommy asked.

"I won't leave until I'm sure. Let's go back up Reynolds and look for him."

Tommy couldn't believe what he was hearing. Here they were—they had made it all the way, free and clear, and Red was talking about going back!

"We can't—" Tommy said.

The bushes behind Saint Paul's stirred, and Henry appeared.

"Henry, it's you," Tommy said.

"Sure is," Henry said.

"You're going to be free," Tommy said.

Henry smiled. "I've been free in Christ. Now I'll be free in this world."

Red peered out of the bushes. "It's clear," he said. "Tommy, thank you." He shook Tommy's hand.

"God bless ya, Master Tommy." Henry turned and made a dash for the trestle.

At that moment, Big Steve rang again. Red smiled. "I bid you farewell with Whittier," he said.

" But blest the ear
That yet shall hear
The jubilant bell
That rings the knell
Of slavery forever."

The train whistle blew, and Red ran for the trestle. That's when Tommy heard his father calling.

CHAPTER 16

Farewell

Tommy peeked out of the bushes. His father and Annie were standing in the middle of the intersection, calling his name. Tommy was never so glad to see anyone. He stepped out and waved. Samson bounded toward Tommy.

"There he is," Annie yelled. She and their father ran toward Tommy. Reverend McKnight's great strides covered the distance in no time.

Tommy looked back, just in time to see Red and Henry disappear inside the tunnel over the trestle. In the moonlight he could see the train chugging its way toward the entrance on the other side, the noise growing louder.

"Hurry, you can make it," Tommy whispered.

Then Annie and their father were there, grabbing up Tommy in a huge hug. Suddenly Tommy felt as tired as a slave picking cotton.

Reverend McKnight relaxed a little and said, "Tommy, I was beside myself when I saw Annie on Broad Street and she told me what happened. You put yourself in danger."

"But, Father, Red is going home to his family in Ohio and Henry's going to be free," Tommy said, relieved to unload the burden.

"Where are they?" Annie asked.

"They're in the tunnel, but I don't know if they made it."

"Perhaps we can see them," Reverend McKnight said. He grabbed Tommy's hand and they hurried to the edge of the Savannah River. The earthy smell of the river and the loud approach of the train engulfed them as they peered into the darkness.

"Can you see them?" Annie yelled.

On the South Carolina side the shadows shifted in the darkness.

Tommy squinted hard. "I can't see anything. Father, can you see them?"

As the train rumbled onto the trestle, grinding noise drowned out his father's response.

Tommy stared into the darkness and remembered the first time he had seen Red: in the bright sun, lying on that pile of dead men, clutching his commonplace book. That was only three days earlier, but it seemed like a lifetime.

It wasn't only for Red's benefit that this had happened. It was for Tommy, too. Just a few days ago mercy was something you talked about in church, not something you actually did.

The train burst out of the tunnel next to them and continued down Washington Street.

"Do you see them?" Reverend McKnight yelled above the noise.

Tommy pointed. "Over there."

"Yes, there they are!" Annie yelled.

Tommy and Annie waved high and hard. One of the shadowy figures lifted a hand in response.

Tommy held his arm out straight, extending his hand high, just like his father did at the end of the church service when he pronounced a blessing on the congregation.

"Father?" Annie asked. "How will they make it all the way to Ohio?"

"I imagine there'll be people who will help them along the way."

"People like us," Tommy said.

"People like you."

"Father, I feel like the last two days have changed everything. I have so much to tell you," Tommy said.

Augusta, Georgia

DECEMBER 1863

Epilogue

The letter arrived on December 1 and was addressed to Thomas McKnight. Tommy's father called him into the study and handed it to him.

"What's this?" Tommy asked.

"A letter for you . . . from Ohio."

As soon as he heard "Ohio," Tommy knew it was from Red.

Tommy opened the envelope and recognized the paper. "It's from his commonplace book."

"Would you like me to read it to you?" asked Reverend McKnight.

Tommy wanted to share the letter with his father. Together they had stood by the river and watched Red and Henry make their final escape. His father had not punished Tommy for sneaking off at night or helping a Yankee escape or any of the other things Tommy had done.

As they walked home, Tommy had told his father about Henry and Red and mercy. Reverend McKnight had said only one thing.

"I admire a person with the courage to follow the leading of God, regardless of whether I agree or not." It was the best compliment he could have given, and Tommy loved him for that.

Tommy handed the page to his father, who read it out loud.

December 1863

Arrived in Ohio to a joyous greeting.
My mother's tears.
My father's strong embrace.
My wife's sweet kiss and the gentle
face of my son.
Henry is well. He works for a small
church not far from here.

My joy is great, as is my appreciation
to a fine Southern gentleman, Thomas
McKnight, and his brave sister Annie,
and his courageous dog, Samson.

God's blessing on you always,

Red

"Freedom is a good thing," Tommy said.

Reverend McKnight nodded. "It is indeed. I have something for you." He opened his desk drawer, pulled out a book, and handed it to Tommy.

"There's no title or author's name," Tommy said, smiling. "A commonplace book."

Reverend McKnight nodded again. "And you can fill it with your own poems and sayings."

"The first thing I'm going to write," Tommy said, "is the story of Red and Henry."

Author's Note

The idea for this story came from the life of Thomas Woodrow Wilson (1856–1924). When he was a year old, his father became pastor of First Presbyterian Church in Augusta, Georgia. They lived across the street in the church manse (the home for the pastor). The church and home still stand today and are open to the public.

As a child, Woodrow Wilson was called Tommy. In law school he began using his middle name, and from then on, he was known as Woodrow. This was his name when he was president of the United States.

Tommy Wilson grew up in a close and loving family. He was a smart child, but did not learn to read until about age eleven. Some experts suggest he was dyslexic. His father taught him at home and coached him in debate. Tommy Wilson and some friends formed the Lightfoot Baseball Club, and Tommy served as president. Tommy's curiosity and hard work enabled him to excel. His Presbyterian faith remained strong throughout his life.

Mountain Boy was Tommy Wilson's greyhound dog. In the Woodrow Wilson house in Augusta, there is a picture that young Tommy drew of Mountain Boy.

Tommy was four years old when the Civil War began. Parades of finely dressed soldiers marched down Broad Street, and citizens cheered as they sent their men off to fight. For the next two years, spirits remained high.

Then the South suffered major defeats at Vicksburg and Gettysburg. Refugees poured into Augusta. Daily, the trains brought in bandaged and bloody soldiers, who hobbled, shuffled, and limped from the railway depot to nearby hospitals.

In the fall of 1863, First Presbyterian Church was converted into a hospital, and Yankee prisoners were kept in the fenced churchyard. Because Tommy Wilson lived across the street, he witnessed firsthand the death and devastation of war.

Everyone in Augusta was involved in the war effort, making bandages, housing the wounded, providing food for the hospitals, donating money and goods. Most of the ammunition for the South was made in Augusta, and one Sunday Tommy's father dismissed church early so the congregation could go to the arsenal and help prepare badly needed ammunition.

There is no information to confirm that Tommy Wilson had contact with any Confederate or Yankee soldiers. However, he must have known soldiers from Augusta, and he likely met a number of other soldiers who were wounded and found themselves in the city.

Tommy Wilson lived only a block from the railroad depot, and this exposed him to much activity. As an adult, he wrote of watching the captured Confederate president, Jefferson Davis, being led in chains from the depot to the Savannah River for the trip to Washington.

He also wrote of meeting Robert E. Lee at the Augusta depot and shaking his hand.

Woodrow Wilson served as president of Princeton University and then governor of New Jersey, so he is thought of by many as the president from New Jersey. But he lived his first eighteen years in the South, thirteen of those in Augusta, Georgia. On October 13, 1904, Woodrow Wilson made this statement:

> *A boy never gets over his boyhood, and never can change those subtle influences which have become a part of him, that were bred in him when he was a child.*

Woodrow Wilson's early impressions of war were evident when he was president of the United States during World War I. He worked diligently for peace and in 1919 was awarded the Nobel Peace Prize.

GOFISH

LAURIE MYERS

Bradley Crosby

What did you want to be when you grew up?
A detective—I loved Nancy Drew. She was a teenage detective, confident and brave, and she could do anything: paint, cook, swim, ride horses, play tennis and golf, drive boats and a car . . . and she was a sharp dresser!

When did you realize you wanted to be a writer?
I always enjoyed writing but never considered doing it as a profession. I was a nurse for ten years, then I had an idea for a book. The idea was begging to be written—so I did.

What's your most embarrassing childhood memory?
During a game of tag on the playground in elementary school, someone accidently grabbed the string to my

wraparound skirt. I kept running and was halfway across the playground before realizing I was in my underwear. That was embarrassing.

What's your favorite childhood memory?
Visiting my grandparents' houses. There was so much to explore—closets and attics and garages and boxes of dress-up clothes and old magazines and interesting books. One set of grandparents lived by a railroad track. Before lunch we would put coins on the tracks, then later run out to pick up the flattened coins. The other grandparents lived in a huge old house with a massive yard, where we'd have picnics and play hide-and-seek.

What was your favorite thing about school?
Math. I love solving problems and was always excited by sheets of math homework.

What were your hobbies as a kid? What are your hobbies now?
My father was an engineer and had a full workshop in the basement. My mother taught us to sew. So we were constantly organizing creative projects and carrying them out—building go-carts and making puppet theaters and sewing costumes. There was always something going on. To this day, I love a project.

Did you play sports as a kid?
Just neighborhood games, like tag and hide-and-seek.

How did you celebrate publishing your first book?

The first celebration occurred the day I received the book in the mail and saw it for the first time. I did a happy dance with my dogs. Later I celebrated with family.

What sparked your imagination for *Escape by Night*?

I was visiting the Woodrow Wilson childhood home in Augusta, Georgia, and was standing in the upstairs room gazing out the window. I imagined what a young boy would have seen—all the soldiers and prisoners going to and coming from the First Presbyterian Church across the street, and all the people from the railroad depot nearby. He was right in the middle of all the activity.

What was the research process like?

I love research. The research for this book started with lots of reading about the Civil War and what was going on in Augusta at the time. Then as I began to write, I continued to look for more details. I spent time wandering around the area where the book takes place: First Presbyterian Church and the Savannah River and St. Paul's Church and Reynolds Street. I walked the route that Tommy takes.

What was the most interesting thing you learned while doing research for the book?

Probably how profoundly the war affected a young Woodrow Wilson. So much so that he constantly sought peace—and later won the Nobel Peace Prize.

SQUARE FISH

Are you a history buff?
I don't think of myself as a history buff, although I find history very interesting.

What historical periods interest you the most?
I find myself more interested in people no matter what the era.

Did you have a dog growing up?
Oh yes. When I was growing up, we always had at least two dogs, sometimes three. As an adult I have always had a dog. Right now it's a whippet named Samson, just like in the book. Most of my books have at least one dog character, and some have many.

What challenges do you face in the writing process, and how do you overcome them?
Sometimes I'm just not sure what should happen next in a story, and there are lots of possibilities. I usually set the story aside and read other things. Reading and writing go hand in hand, and one stimulates the other.

Which of your characters is most like you?
The dogs.

What's your favorite song?
I love "Stars and Stripes Forever" by John Philip Sousa. Peppy and fun, it always makes me smile. My high school band played it every year, and I played flute. The flute part in that song is fun to play.

What was your favorite book when you were a kid?
Charlotte's Web and *Old Yeller*—anything with animals.

Do you have a favorite book now?
As a Christian, I'd have to say the Bible—filled with drama and so many great stories.

What's your favorite TV show or movie?
We don't have cable, so I don't watch much TV. I loved the movie *Babe*.

If you could travel anywhere in the world, where would you go and what would you do?
I love the beach, so I would choose a beautiful sandy beach. Then I would do lots of beach activities—build a sand castle, read a book, swim in the ocean, sit in the surf, and anything else I felt like doing.

What's the best advice you have ever received about writing?
Write—write—write.

SQUARE FISH